C0-ATW-266

Chicka Chicka Boom Boom

Published by arrangement with
SIMON AND SCHUSTER BOOKS FOR YOUNG READERS
a Division of Simon & Schuster Inc., New York

SRA
Macmillan/McGraw-Hill

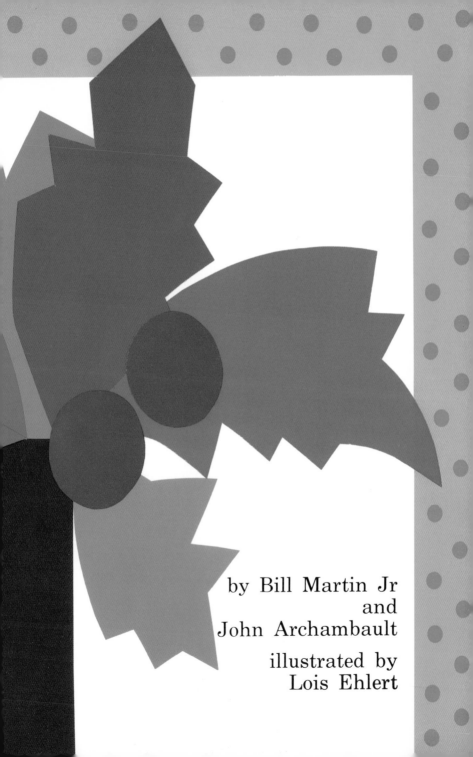

by Bill Martin Jr
and
John Archambault

illustrated by
Lois Ehlert

A told **B**,
and **B** told **C**,
"I'll meet you at the top
of the coconut tree."

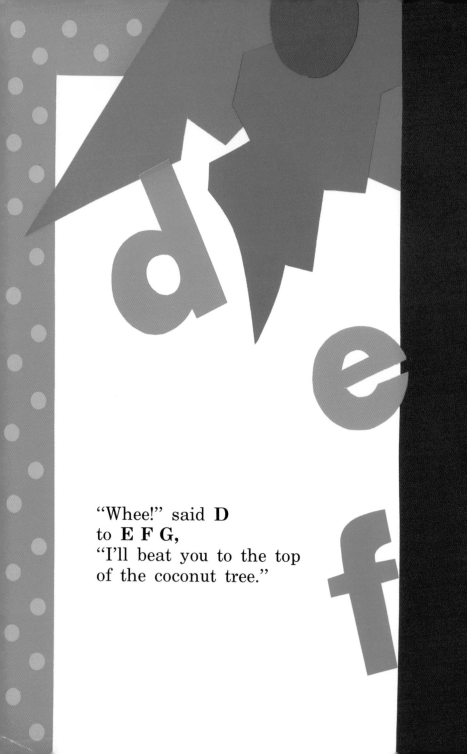

"Whee!" said **D**
to **E F G,**
"I'll beat you to the top
of the coconut tree."

Chicka chicka boom boom!
Will there be enough room?
Here comes **H**
up the coconut tree,

and **I** and **J**
and tag-along **K,**
all on their way
up the coconut tree.

Chicka chicka boom boom!
Will there be enough room?
Look who's coming!
L M N O P!

And **Q R S!**

And **T U V**!

Still more—**W!**
And **X Y Z!**

The whole alphabet
up the—Oh, no!

Chicka chicka...
BOOM! BOOM!

Skit skat skoodle doot
Flip flop flee.
Everybody running to the coconut tree.
Mamas and papas
and uncles and aunts
hug their little dears,
then dust their pants.

"Help us up!"
cried **A B C.**

Next from the pileup
skinned-knee **D**
and stubbed-toe **E**
and patched-up **F,**
then comes **G**
all out of breath.

H is tangled up with **I**.
J and **K** are about to cry.
L is knotted like a tie.

M is looped.
N is stooped.
O is twisted alley-oop.
Skit skat skoodle doot
Flip flop flee...

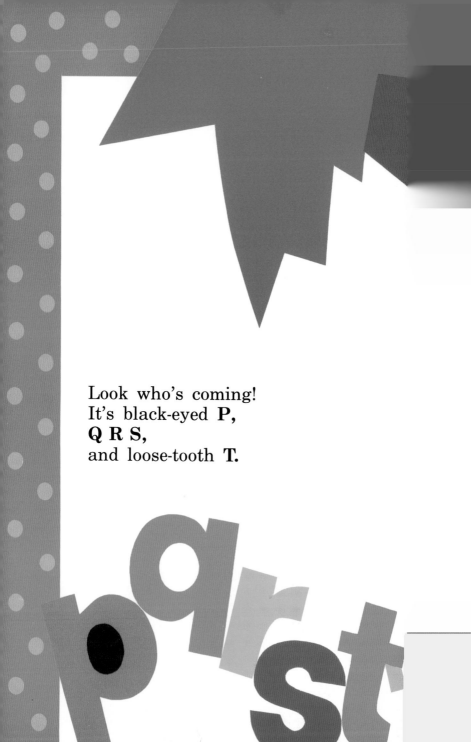

Look who's coming!
It's black-eyed **P,**
Q R S,
and loose-tooth **T.**

Then **U V W**
wiggle-jiggle free.

Last to come
X Y Z,

And the sun goes down
on the coconut tree...

But—
chicka chicka boom boom!
Look, there's a full moon.

A is out of bed,
and this is what he said,
"Dare double dare,
you can't catch me.
I'll beat you to the top
of the coconut tree."
Chicka chicka
BOOM! BOOM!

The
DLM®
Legacy
Collection
of
Children's
Literature

The DLM Legacy Collection of Children's Literature

The Bear with Golden Hair by Karla Kuskin
Chicka Chicka Boom Boom by Bill Martin Jr and John Archambault
The Itsy Bitsy Spider Nursery Rhyme
Mouse, Frog, and Little Red Hen Folk Tale
Twickham Tweer by Jack Prelutsky
What Can You Do with a Pocket? by Eve Merriam

For Arie Alexander Archambault, new baby boom boom—JA

For Libby and Liza, Helen and Morris—LE

Text copyright © 1989 by Bill Martin Jr and John Archambault
Illustrations copyright © 1989 by Lois Ehlert
All rights reserved including the right of reproduction
in whole or in part in any form.
Published by arrangement with
SIMON AND SCHUSTER BOOKS FOR YOUNG READERS
ISBN 1-55294-577-8

3 4 5 6 7 8 9   97 96 95 94 93

Chicka Chicka Boom Boom

AaBbC
FfGgH
LlMmN
QqRrS
VvWwX